MIKE YOUNG

SUPERTED
RETURNS TO CREEPY CASTLE

Illustrations by Tony Hutchings

Frederick Muller Limited
London

A storm rages over the mountains of Eastern Europe. Through the rain and darkness of night, three bank robbers are making their way to their hide-out . . . the evil Creepy Castle.

Thousands of miles away safe in their tree-house, SuperTed, his extra-terrestrial friend Spottyman and Spottyman's spotty teddy bear are dozing their way through a warm summer's afternoon. Suddenly they are awakened by the bleep of their video scanner.

A little girl with blond plaits is trying to contact SuperTed. She quickly explains that her father, the caretaker of a deserted castle , has disappeared and nobody dares follow him . . . the castle is haunted.

The bear whispers his special magic word which only he knows and becomes SuperTed. Spottyman straps on his rocket-pack. They are soon zooming through a terrible electrical storm towards Creepy Castle, when SuperTed shouts a warning.

"Galloping Gooseberries! Be careful Spotty or you might be struck by lightning." Whizzing over a steep mountain ridge they see Creepy Castle. Spottyman thinks he has never seen anything quite as spooky before.

The three villains, Bulk, Skeleton and Texas Pete have decided that Creepy Castle would provide the ideal place for hiding their stolen loot. The wicked Texan is delighted.

"You won't believe this Skeleton, but the superstitious villagers think this place is haunted."

Skeleton moves a little closer to Tex and asks, "I don't suppose you'd mind if I held your hand, would you Tex?"

"Yes, I would," growls Tex.

Bulk is a little kinder, "You can hold my hand if you like Skeleton."

Tex laughs his evil laugh. "Ha! Ha! Hey, I don't know what you're worried about . . . there's no ghost here." At that very moment their candles are blown out.

Meanwhile SuperTed and Spottyman have entered the castle and are searching through the ghostly rooms. SuperTed is a little unsure. "This place makes my fur stand on end. I'm sure someone has been here, there are definite signs of life."

"Don't you mean death?" shivers a very frightened Spottyman. Just then they hear a croaky noise coming from the massive fireplace and decide to investigate.

Spottyman and SuperTed creep forward and carefully step into the fireplace, "I can't see anything," whispers Spottyman.

SuperTed is puzzled, "Well someone has been here before us. Spotty, look! Money! I think this place is being used as a hideout." Suddenly a slab of stone falls, trapping them in the chimney.

Texas Pete stumbles down a steep staircase in total darkness, fumbles for his matches and relights his candles. "This must be the wine cellar. Now where are those numbskulls? Bulk! Skeleton! Hey, you don't think the ghost has got them? No, I forgot, I don't believe in ghosts."

Bulk and Skeleton peep out of two large wine barrels and Tex kicks the barrels in anger. "Get out you idiots."

Skeleton complains. "I'm coming, I'm coming. There's no need to shout, just tasting the wine, it's got a dry fruity taste with just a . . ."

Tex loses his temper, "Come out and shut up."

As they leave the cellar another pair of ghostly eyes peep out of a third barrel.

Inside the chimney SuperTed and Spottyman find a narrow shaft which leads downwards. Beneath them there is a faint chink of light. They decide to climb down and soon hear a strange moaning sound. They carry on down, both our heroes feeling a little nervous. The moaning gets louder. SuperTed listens unhappily, "It sort of churns your stuffing."

They arrive in a scary room full of weird looking carvings and statues.

"Look", says Spotty, "that must be the girl's father." They find the caretaker who had been tied up with a cowboy lasso.

Just then the baddies arrive in a doorway, "Look there Spotty, the biggest horror of all . . . it's Texas Pete."

Tex growls, "Come and get me, you mangy little teddy."

SuperTed zooms forward. "You don't have to ask me twice, Texas Pete."

Tex throws his lasso and ropes SuperTed who, with an enormous heave, swings the crooked cowboy off his feet. Then with a flick of the wrist, he spins Tex around with his own lasso until he's trussed up like a turkey. Meanwhile, Spottyman has had no trouble from Bulk and Skeleton. They have been frightened stiff by a huge stuffed alligator.

Outside the castle SuperTed has reunited the caretaker with his pretty daughter.

"Well that's another mystery wound up. We'll leave Texas Pete, Bulk and Skeleton in the castle for the night and collect them in the morning."

As SuperTed and Spottyman speed into the now clear sky, the happy caretaker cuddles his daughter, saying, "I knew if I moaned long enough, someone would come to help, but it was very nasty in there."

The pretty little girl asks, "Did Texas Pete and all those horrible statues frighten you in there?"

"No, no," replies the caretaker, "Zat was nothing my child, zat is not what frightened me."
"Oh! What then?" she wonders.
Zat ghost of course. It was horrible."